"Just living is not enough . . . one must have sunshine, freedom, and a little flower."
– Hans Christian Andersen

For little flowers everywhere ~ C.C.

For Eliza, may your journeys be full of adventure ~ S.J.

tiger tales
5 River Road, Suite 128, Wilton, CT 06897
Published in the United States 2019
Originally published in Great Britain 2019
by Little Tiger Press Ltd.
Text by Camila Correa
Text copyright © 2019 Little Tiger Press Ltd.
Illustrations copyright © 2019 Sean Julian
ISBN-13: 978-1-68010-128-7
ISBN-10: 1-68010-128-5
Printed in China
LTP/1400/2403/0918

For more insight and activities,
visit us at www.tigertalesbooks.com

Follow Me, Little Fox

A Journey Back to Nature

by
Camila Correa

Illustrated by
Sean Julian

tiger tales

Little Fox loved his city home.
But sometimes, it could be a little too fast,
a bit too busy, and a touch too noisy.

"I know what you need," said Mommy
Fox. "Let's go back to nature."
"What is nature?" asked Little Fox,
who had never gone far from their den.
"Let me show you," said Mommy.

"Nature is the place where the city ends and the wild begins. Where grays and silvers turn green and blue, where birds sing and flowers bloom.

"Nature smells of rain-soaked soil, of fresh sweet petals and sun-drenched grass.

"It is the sound of buzzing bees, whispering leaves, and babbling brooks.

"Nature can be wild and scary . . .

". . . and yet it is full of the most magical surprises!

Here, we are free to roam, to play, to splash . . .

and to HOWL!

AAAAOOOOOOOO!

"Nature is the joy you feel when you race up a hill, and your heart beats faster with every step!"

Little Fox didn't want the day to end.
"Can we stay out here tonight, under
the moon and stars?" he asked.
"Yes," smiled Mommy. "But
those aren't stars . . .

". . . they are the twinkling city lights."
Little Fox watched the lights dance
on the horizon. He felt the warm
evening breeze against his fur and
the cool earth beneath his feet.

"I'm going to miss nature," he yawned.
"Maybe you won't have to," said Mommy.
And together, they came up with a plan.

Every time Little Fox and his mommy visited nature,
they brought back seeds for the city.

Soon, others began to do the same.
And those seeds grew and grew, just like Little Fox . . .

. . . until their home looked
wonderful.